Dinah M. M. Craik

It is the Christmas-Time

Dinah M. M. Craik

It is the Christmas-Time

ISBN/EAN: 9783337380601

Printed in Europe, USA, Canada, Australia, Japan

Cover: Foto ©Andreas Hilbeck / pixelio.de

More available books at **www.hansebooks.com**

IT IS THE CHRISTMAS-TIME

BY MISS MULOCK

WITH TWELVE IDEAL CHRISTMAS HYMNS AND POEMS

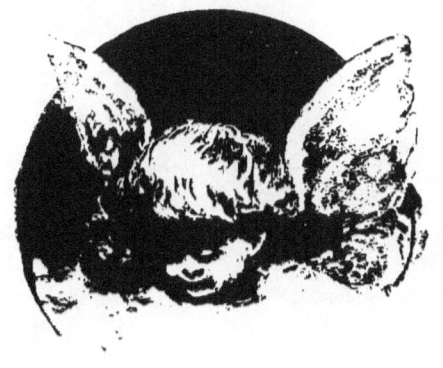

ILLUSTRATED

BOSTON
D. LOTHROP AND COMPANY
FRANKLIN AND HAWLEY STREETS

Press of Berwick & Smith, 118 Purchase Street.

CONTENTS.

A Hymn for Christmas Morning .	*Miss Mulock.*
While Shepherds Watched Their Flocks by Night	*Nahum Tate.*
Hark! The Herald Angels Sing	. *Charles Wesley.*
The Star Song .	*Robert Herrick.*
Epiphany	. *Reginald Heber.*
A Christmas Hymn	*John Keble.*
The Angel's Song	*Rev. E. H. Sears.*
The Angels .	*William Drummond.*
A Christmas Vision	*James Montgomery.*
The Christmas Carol.	. *William Wordsworth.*
Mary's Song	*George MacDonald.*
The Wild-Fowl's Voice	*Charles Kingsley.*
A Christmas Carmen. (By permission of Houghton, Mifflin & Co.) .	*John G. Whittier.*

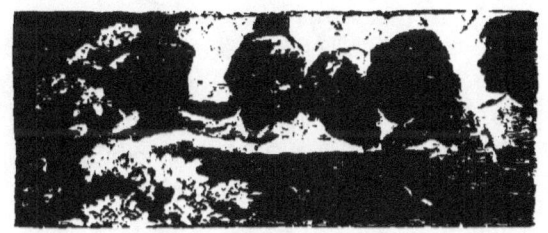

"IT IS THE CHRISTMAS-TIME."

A HYMN FOR CHRISTMAS MORNING.

It is the Christmas-time:
And up and down 'twixt heaven and earth
In glorious grief and solemn mirth,
    The shining angels climb.

    And unto everything
That lives and moves, for heaven, on earth,
With equal share of grief and mirth,
    The shining angels sing: —

    " Babes new-born, undefiled,
In lowly hut, or mansion wide —
Sleep safely through this Christmas-tide
    When Jesus was a child.

    " O young men, bold and free,
In peopled town or desert grim,
When ye are tempted like to Him,
    'The man Christ Jesus' see.

"Poor mothers, with your hoard
Of endless love and countless pain —
Remember all her grief, her gain.
   The Mother of the Lord.

"Mourners, half blind with woe,
Look up! One standeth in his place,
And by the pity of his face
   The Man of Sorrows know.

"Wanderers in far countrie.
O think of Him who came, forgot,
To His own, and they received Him not —
   Jesus of Galilee.

"O all ye who have trod
The wine-press of affliction, lay
Your hearts before His heart this day —
   Behold the Christ of God!"

                — *Miss Mulock.*

"WANDERERS IN FAR COUNTRIE."

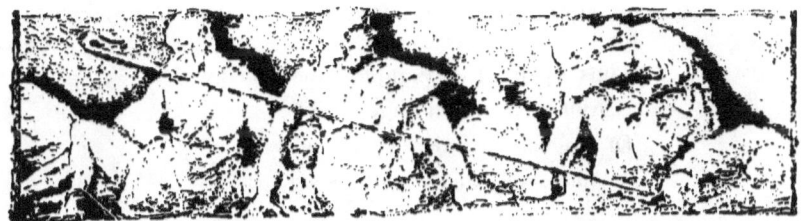

"WHILE SHEPHERDS WATCHED THEIR FLOCKS BY NIGHT."

WHILE SHEPHERDS WATCHED THEIR FLOCKS BY NIGHT.

While shepherds watch'd their flocks by night.
  All seated on the ground.
The angel of the Lord came down.
  And glory shone around.

"Fear not," said he; (for mighty dread
  Had seized their troubled mind;)
"Glad tidings of great joy I bring
  To you and all mankind.

"To you in David's town this day
  Is born of David's line
The Saviour. who is Christ the Lord;
  And this shall be the sign.

"The Heavenly Babe you there shall find
  To human view displayed.
All meanly wrapt in swathing bands,
  And in a manger laid."

Thus spake the Seraph; and forthwith
   Appeared a shining throng
Of angels, praising God, and thus
   Addressed their joyful song.

" All glory be to God on high,
   And to the earth be peace;
Good will henceforth from Heaven to men
   Begin, and never cease!"

— Nahum Tate.

"AND TO THE EARTH BE PEACE."

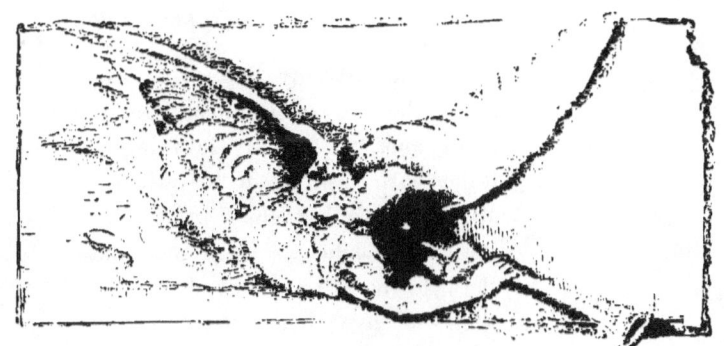

"HARK! THE HERALD ANGELS SING."

HARK! THE HERALD ANGELS SING.

Hark! the herald angels sing,
"Glory to the new-born King:
Peace on earth, and mercy mild,
God and sinners reconciled!"
Joyful all ye nations, rise,
Join the triumph of the skies;
Universal nature, say,
Christ the Lord is born to-day!

Christ, by highest Heaven adored;
Christ, the Everlasting Lord;
Late in time behold Him come,
Offspring of a Virgin's womb;
Veiled in flesh the Godhead see,
Hail, th' Incarnate Deity,
Pleased as man with men to appear,
Jesus our Immanuel here!

Hail! the heavenly Prince of Peace!
Hail! the son of Righteousness!
Light and life to all He brings,
Risen with healing in his wings.
Mild he lays his glory by,
Born that man no more may die.
Born to raise the sons of earth.
Born to give them second birth.

Come, Desire of nations, come.
Fix in us thy humble home.
Rise, the woman's conquering seed,
Bruise in us the Serpent's head.
Now display thy saving power,
Ruined nature now restore.
Now in mystic union join
Thine to ours, and ours to thine.

Adam's likeness, Lord, efface;
Stamp thy image in its place;
Second Adam from above,
Reinstate us in Thy love.
Let us Thee, though lost, regain.
Thee, the Life, the Heavenly Man:
O. to all Thy self impart,
Formed in each believing heart!

— *Charles Wesley.*

THE STAR-SONG.

Tell us, thou clear and heavenly tongue,
Where is the Babe but lately sprung?
Lies he the lily-banks among?

Or say, if this new Birth of ours
Sleeps, laid within some ark of flowers.
Spangled with dew-light; thou canst clear
All doubts, and manifest the where.

Declare to us, bright star, if we shall seek
Him in the morning's blushing cheek.
Or search the beds of spices through,
To find him out?

STAR: No, this ye need not do;
But only come and see Him rest.
A princely babe, on 's mother's breast.
— *Robert Herrick.*

EPIPHANY.

Brightest and best of the sons of the morning,
   Dawn on our darkness and lend us thine aid!
Star of the east, the horizon adorning,
   Guide where our infant Redeemer is laid!

Cold on His cradle the dew-drops are shining,
   Low lies His bed with the beasts of the stall;
Angels adore Him in slumber reclining —
   Maker, and monarch, and Saviour of all.

Say, shall we yield him in costly devotion,
   Odors of Edom, and offerings divine:
Gems of the mountain and pearls of the ocean;
   Myrrh from the forest and gold from the mine?

Vainly we offer each ample oblation,
   Vainly with gold would His favor secure;
Richer by far is the heart's adoration,
   Dearer to God are the prayers of the poor.

Brightest and best of the sons of the morning,
   Dawn on our darkness and lend us thine aid!
Star of the east, the horizon adorning,
   Guide where our infant Redeemer is laid!

                            — Reginald Heber.

"GUIDE WHERE OUR INFANT REDEEMER IS LAID."

"UPON A CLEAR BLUE RIVER."

A CHRISTMAS HYMN.

What sudden blaze of song
    Spreads o'er the expanse of Heaven?
  In waves of light it thrills along,
    Th' angelic signal given:
Glory to God! from yonder central fire
Flows out the echoing lay beyond the starry choir.

    Like circles widening round
      Upon a clear blue river.
    Orb after orb, the wondrous sound
      Is echoed on forever:
"Glory to God on high, on earth be peace.
And love toward men of love, salvation and release!"

    Yet stay, before thou dare
      To join that festal throng;
    Listen, and mark what gentle air
      First stirred the tide of song:
'T is not, "the Saviour born in David's home,
To whom for power and health obedient worlds should come."

'T is not. "the Christ the Lord":
 With fixed adoring look
The choir of angels caught the word,
 Nor yet their silence broke:
But when they heard the sign. where Christ should be,
In sudden light they shone, and heavenly harmony.

 Wrapped in His swaddling bands,
  And in his manger laid,
 The Hope and Glory of all lands
  Is come to the world's aid:
No peaceful home upon His cradle smiled;
Guests rudely went and came. where slept the royal Child.

 But where Thou dwellest. Lord,
  No other thought should be;
 Once duly welcomed and adored.
  How should I part with Thee?
Bethlehem must lose Thee soon; but Thou wilt grace
The single heart to be Thy sure abiding-place.

 Thee, on the bosom laid
  Of a pure virgin mind.
 In quiet ever and in shade
  Shepherd and sage may find;
They, who have bowed untaught to nature's sway,
And they, who follow Truth along her star-paved way.

 The pastoral spirits first
  Approach Thee, Babe divine;

"BETHLEHEM MUST LOSE THEE SOON."

For they in lonely thoughts are nurst,
　　Meet for thy lowly shrine;
Sooner than they should miss where Thou dost dwell,
Angels from Heaven will stoop to guide them to Thy cell.

　　Still as the day comes round
　　For Thee to be revealed,
　　By wakeful shepherds thou art found,
　　Abiding in the field:
All through the wintry heaven and chill night air
In music and in light Thou dawnest on their prayer.

"YOUR WANDERING SHEEP!"

　　O faint not ye for fear!
　　What though your wandering sheep,
　　Reckless of what they see and hear,
　　Lie lost in wilful sleep?
High Heaven, in mercy to your sad annoy,
Still greets you with glad tidings of immortal joy.

Think on the eternal home
  The Saviour left for you;
Think on the Lord most holy, come
  To dwell with hearts untrue:
So shall ye tread untried His pastoral ways,
And in the darkness sing your carol of high praise.

—John Keble.

THE ANGEL'S SONG.

It came upon the midnight clear,
  That glorious song of old.
From angels bending near the earth,
  To touch their harps of gold:
"Peace on earth, good will to men.
  From Heaven's all-gracious King."
The world in solemn stillness lay
  To hear the angels sing.

Still thro' the cloven skies they come,
  With peaceful wings unfurled;
And still their heavenly music floats
  O'er all the weary world:

"AND YE BENEATH LIFE'S CRUSHING LOAD."

THE ANGEL'S SONG.

Above its sad and lowly plains
   They bend on hovering wing,
And ever o'er its Babel sounds
   The blessed angels sing.

But with the woes of sin and strife
   The world has suffered long;
Beneath the angel-strain have rolled
   Two thousand years of wrong;
And man, at war with man, hears not
   The love-song which they bring:
O hush the noise, ye men of strife,
   And hear the angels sing.

And ye, beneath life's crushing load
   Whose forms are bending low,
Who toil along the climbing way,
   With painful steps and slow —
Look now: for glad and golden hours
   Come swiftly on the wing:
O rest beside the weary road,
   And hear the angels sing.

For lo, the days are hastening on
   By prophet bards foretold,
When with the ever circling years
   Comes round the age of gold

When Peace shall over all the earth
   Its ancient splendors fling,
And the whole world give back the song
   Which now the angels sing.

                — Rev. E. H. Sears.

THE ANGELS.

Run, shepherds, run where Bethlehem blest appears.
   We bring the best of news; be not dismayed :
A Saviour there is born more old than years.
   Amidst Heaven's rolling height this earth who stayed,
In a poor cottage inned, a virgin maid
   A weakling did him bear, who all upbears;
There is he poorly swaddled, in manger laid,
   To whom too narrow swaddlings are our spheres :
Run, shepherds, run, and solemnize his birth.
   This is that night — no, day, grown great with bliss,
   In which the power of Satan broken is :
In Heaven be glory, peace unto the earth !
   Thus singing, through the air the angels swarm,
   And cope of stars re-echoed the same.

                — Drummond.

"A SAVIOUR THERE IS BORN."

"THE STRANGER MEEK AND LOWLY."

A CHRISTMAS VISION.

The scene around me disappears,
  And, borne to ancient regions,
While time recalls the flight of years,
  I see angelic legions
Descending in an orb of light:
Amidst the dark and solemn night
  I hear celestial voices.

Tidings, glad tidings from above
　　To every age and nation!
Tidings, glad tidings! God is Love,
　　To man He sends salvation!
His Son beloved, His only Son,
The work of mercy hath begun;
　　Give to His Name the glory!

Through David's city I am led;
　　Here all around are sleeping;
A light directs to yon poor shed;
　　There lonely watch is keeping:
I enter; ah! what glories shine!
Is this Immanuel's earthly shrine,
　　Messiah's infant Temple?

It is, it is; and I adore
　　This Stranger meek and lowly,
As saints and angels bow before
　　The throne of God thrice Holy!
Faith through the veil of flesh can see
The face of Thy Divinity,
　　My Lord, my God, my Saviour!
　　　　　　　　—James Montgomery.

THE CHRISTMAS CAROL.

The minstrels played their Christmas tune
  To-night beneath my cottage eaves;
While, smitten by a lofty moon,
  The encircling laurels, thick with leaves,
Gave back a rich and dazzling sheen,
That overpowered their natural green.

Through hill and valley every breeze
  Had sunk to rest with folded wings:
Keen was the air, but could not freeze,
  Nor check, the music of the strings;
So stout and hearty were the band
That scraped the chords with strenuous hand!

And who but listened? — till was paid
  Respect to every inmate's claim:
The greeting given, the music played,
  In honor of each household name,
Duly pronounced with lusty call,
And " Merry Christmas" wished to all!

How touching, when, at midnight, sweep
  Snow-muffled winds and all is dark,
To hear, and sink again to sleep!

Or, at an earlier call, to mark,
By blazing fire, the still suspense
Of self-complacent innocence;

The mutual nod,— the grave disguise
  Of hearts with gladness brimming o'er;
And some unbidden tears that rise
  For names once heard, and heard no more;
Tears brightened by the serenade
For infant in the cradle laid.

Hail, ancient Manners! sure defence,
  Where they survive, of wholesome laws;
Remnants of love whose modest sense
  Thus into narrow room withdraws;
Hail, usages of pristine mould,
And ye that guard them, Mountains old!
                — *William Wordsworth.*

WITHIN THE COTTAGE.

MARY'S SONG.

Babe Jesus lay in Mary's lap;
  The sun shone on his hair:
And this was how she saw, mayhap,
  The crown already there.

For she sang: " Sleep on, my little king,
  Bad Herod dares not come;
Before thee sleeping, holy thing,
  The wild winds would be dumb.

" I kiss thy hands, I kiss thy feet,
  My child, so long desired;
Thy hands shall never be soiled, my sweet;
  Thy feet shall never be tired.

" For thou art the king of men, my son;
  Thy crown I see it plain;
And men shall worship thee, every one,
  And cry. Glory! Amen!"

Babe Jesus opened his eyes so wide!
  At Mary looked her Lord.
And Mary stinted her song and sighed.
  Babe Jesus said never a word.

                              — *George MacDonald.*

THE WILD FOWL'S VOICE.

It chanced upon the merry, merry Christmas eve,
  I went sighing past the church across the moorland dreary—
O, never sin and want and woe this earth will leave,
  And the bells but mock the wailing sound, they sing so
    cheery.

How long, O Lord! how long before Thou come again?
  Still in cellar, and in garret, and on mountain dreary.
The orphans moan, and widows weep, and poor men toil in vain,
  Till earth is sick of hope deferred, though Christmas bells
    be cheery.

Then arose a joyous clamor from the wild-fowl on the mere,
  Beneath the stars, across the snow, like clear bells ringing,
And a voice within cried — " Listen! — Christmas carols even
    here
Though thou be dumb, yet o'er their work the stars and
    snows are singing.

" Blind! I live, I love, I reign; and all the nations through,
  With the thunder of My judgments even now are ringing;
Do thou fulfil thy work but as you wild-fowl do,
  Thou wilt heed no less the wailing, yet hear through it
    angels singing."

— *Charles Kingsley.*

"I LIVE, I LOVE, I REIGN!"

"HOPE OF THE AGES."

A CHRISTMAS CARMEN.

Sound over all waters, reach out from all lands,
The chorus of voices, the clasping of hands;
Sing hymns that were sung by the stars of the morn,
Sing songs of the angels when Jesus was born!
       With glad jubilations
       Bring hope to the nations!
The dark night is ending and dawn is begun;
Rise. hope of the ages, arise like the sun,
All speech flow to music, all hearts beat as one!

Sing the bridal of nations! with chorals of love
Sing out the war-vulture and sing in the dove,

"SING THE SONG OF GREAT JOY."

Till the hearts of the peoples keep time in accord,
And the voice of the world is the voice of the Lord!
     Clasp hands of the nations
     In strong gratulations:

A CHRISTMAS CARMEN.

The dark night is ending and dawn has begun;
Rise, hope of the ages, arise like the sun,
All speech flow to music, all hearts beat as one!

Blow, bugles of battle, the marches of peace;
East, west, north and south let the long quarrel cease:
Sing the song of great joy that the angels began,
Sing of glory to God and of good will to man!
   Hark! joining in chorus
    The heavens bend o'er us!
The dark night is ending and dawn has begun;
Rise, hope of the ages, arise like the sun,
All speech flow to music, all hearts beat as one!
        —J. G. Whittier.